# YOUR CHOICE

## A Personal Skills Course

# A GUIDE TO YOUR CHOICE: MAKING ACTIVE LEARNING WORK
## Shay McConnon

## ACKNOWLEDGEMENTS

Producing this series has involved a lot of people in a variety of ways. My thanks to friends and colleagues who have encouraged and supported me in developing the work, in particular my wife, whose interest and enthusiasm has fired my own.

I would like to thank Alan Booth, Hampshire County Adviser for Personal and Social Education; David Hogg, Deputy Principal Psychologist, Hampshire; Ginny Straugheir, Religious Experience Project, University of Nottingham; the staff and pupils of Buckland School; Brian McQuoid, friend and working colleague; and Miranda Carter, Macmillan, for their time, encouragement, professionalism and friendship.

I am particularly grateful to all the students who experienced this course as it was being developed. Together we laughed, experienced honesty and grew closer together.

Many influences have contributed to this series – books have been read, courses attended and there has been lots of talking. Ideas have evolved, changed and been adapted. I wish to acknowledge all these influences and trust that what is offered in these pages reflects the ideals we share.

Shay McConnon

To Mags. Thanks for the sharing.

© Shay McConnon 1989

All rights reserved. No reproduction, copy or transmission of this publication may be made without written permission.

No paragraph of this publication may be reproduced, copied or transmitted save with written permission or in accordance with the provisions of the Copyright, Designs and Patents Act 1988, or under the terms of any licence permitting limited copying issued by the Copyright Licensing Agency, 33–4 Alfred Place, London WC1E 7DP.

The photocopying of some pages is permitted. These pages are marked thus ℗. However, only reasonable quantities of photocopies can be made and these should be for internal school use only. Under no circumstances can large numbers of copies be made either by schools or LEAs.

Any person who does any unauthorised act in relation to this publication may be liable to criminal prosecution and civil claims for damages.

First published 1989
Reprinted 1990

Published by
MACMILLAN EDUCATION LTD
Houndmills, Basingstoke, Hampshire RG21 2XS
and London
Companies and representatives
throughout the world

Printed in Hong Kong

British Library Cataloguing in Publication Data
McConnon, Shay
Your choice: a personal skills course
1. Life skills
I. Title
305.2'3   HM132
ISBN 0–333–46425–7

# CONTENTS

1 The Nature and Contents of **YOUR CHOICE** ... 1
   What is **YOUR CHOICE**? ... 1
   Aims of **YOUR CHOICE** ... 1
   Who Will Find it Useful? ... 1
   What **YOUR CHOICE** Contains ... 1
   How the Books are Organised ... 2

2 Group-Based Work ... 3
   Ground Rules ... 3
   Breaking into Groups ... 3
   Types of Activities ... 4
   Group Development ... 5
   Energisers ... 7
   Difficulties ... 8

3 The Role of the Teacher ... 10
   Questions and Answers ... 11

Booklist ... 12

# PREFACE

Teachers are increasingly being asked to contribute to the personal and social education of pupils, whether it be in subject lessons or tutorial work. In the sixties and seventies it was expected that a national project or pack would provide the materials and the training; but now it is much more likely that teachers will look for resources that best meet the needs of the pupils and staff in their own particular school. Teachers are more skilled in working out a sequential programme of learning objectives in personal and social development, and pupils and parents are often included in the choice of content and the evaluation of the programmes. It is becoming less likely that personal and social is left to be caught rather than taught.

This series by Shay McConnon can be used in a wide range of contexts. The teacher can take one topic and pursue it in some depth, or select parts of topics to complement existing courses. The group skills work contained in the booklets provide useful preparation for pupils in many areas of school life, including the start of any new group: subjects in which active learning methods are important: person-centred work such as health education and careers education: and experience in the community or in industry. Because of the personal nature of the material, it is always helpful to practise activities with colleagues before using it with pupils.

If you think it is important to encourage young people to establish inner controls rather than blind adherence to outer controls, raise their self-esteem rather than emphasise a sense of failure and dependency, improve confidence in their ability to work, relate and tackle conflict positively with others, then I am sure that these materials will find a valuable place in your programmes.

Shay is a full-time teacher and also part of a team of Hampshire trainers. He has helped many teachers to devise programmes of personal and social education, and also to gain confidence in the skills of using active learning methods. He introduces to all ages that which he is constantly rediscovering for himself, that learning is an exciting process which at its best involves people in becoming more fully themselves; and that such learning leads to a sense of extra purpose, relevance and meaning in life.

Few would argue that we live in settled times or that the future is predictable. Whichever way the educational pendulum swings in response to political or social trends, there will always be a need for active, participative, adaptable young people with clear values, personal ideals and a sense of joy. This publication offers some ways in which the teacher can engage with young people in this developmental process.

Alan R. Booth
Hampshire County General Adviser for Personal and Social Education

# 1 THE NATURE AND CONTENTS OF *YOUR CHOICE*

## What is YOUR CHOICE?

**YOUR CHOICE** is a series of books designed for Personal and Social Education and tutorial work in schools, colleges and youth groups. It may also be used as a flexible component of a Health Education, Religious Education or English course.

The series has been developed and used with young people (11–16+), of mixed ability, in mainstream schools, special schools and Youth Training Schemes. Each book contains strategies on a specific aspect of personal development, and constitutes about a term's work. Alternatively, the materials can be used to complement other PSE materials and teaching.

## Aims of YOUR CHOICE

The series is designed to provide opportunities for improved self-awareness and the development of personal and interpersonal skills. More specifically **YOUR CHOICE** aims:
○ To encourage young people to see their own strengths and to develop a more positive self-image;
○ To develop their listening skills;
○ To encourage them to discover ways of dealing with difficult emotional and social situations;
○ To help them to become aware of how people interact in groups;
○ To heighten awareness of their current behaviour, values and attitudes;
○ To encourage 'ownership' of feelings, values and behaviour;
○ To direct them to strategies for changing behaviour and achieving personal goals.

## Who Will Find it Useful?

The series is primarily intended to complement PSE, Health Education, Religious Education and tutorial work programmes in schools and colleges. It will also be found useful in those subjects which contain an oral/aural component.

Educational psychologists and others who see the value of creating special groups in schools or elsewhere, for young people with social and emotional problems, can use the series as a resource for programmes that lead to behavioural awareness and personal change.

Special schools that cater for deprived and skill-deficient young people can use the series to promote emotional and social growth and extend the young person's repertoire of behavioural skills.

Social workers involved with group work and Intermediate Treatment will find the ideas and strategies helpful in promoting attitudes and skills which may help young offenders to avoid further criminal behaviour.

The strategies are suitable for use in youth clubs as part of the club's activity programmes and for training youth leaders. The course has successfully been used as part of the Social and Lifeskills section of the Youth Training Scheme (YTS) and the Certificate of Pre-Vocational Education (CPVE), and also in programmes with long- to medium-term unemployed adults.

The strategies are broadly suitable for mixed ability groups. The experience and the value to the participants will be different for each group, as each person brings to the learning situation his or her own experiences and levels of awareness.

## What YOUR CHOICE Contains

**THE NATURE OF FRIENDSHIP** aims to help students to understand what friendship is and to explore the qualities and behaviours which foster good relations between people. Students are encouraged to apply what they learn to everyday relationships.

**THE SKILLS OF FRIENDSHIP** follows on from **THE NATURE OF FRIENDSHIP** and deals with some of the skills that are important for successful relationships. Opportunities are provided for students to practise these skills with the aim of integrating them into existing relationships.

**BOYFRIENDS, GIRLFRIENDS** is the third book in a course on friendship, and helps students to discover the importance of friendship and its skills for successful relationships between the sexes. Gender issues and stereotyped attitudes are also explored.

**SELF-ESTEEM** offers students a variety of structured experiences designed to enhance their self-esteem and awareness of how they can be more positive about themselves and others. Students also explore the skills involved in handling positive comments and coping with rejection.

**SELF-AWARENESS** aims to help students to perceive themselves more accurately, to be clearer about life-goals and to make a start in achieving them. Students are encouraged to take responsibility for themselves, their decisions, behaviours and feelings, and hence to take a greater control over their lives.

**INTERPERSONAL COMMUNICATION** provides opportunities for students to practise the skills involved in successful communication between people. Students are encouraged to integrate these into existing relationships.

**ASSERTION** helps students to become aware of themselves as aggressive, passive or assertive in their responses. The consequences of these behaviours are explored and students have the opportunity of identifying alternative ways of behaving.

**CONFLICT** helps students to look at how conflict arises and how to manage it. Opportunities are provided for students to practise the skills of conflict resolution.

## How the Books are Organised

Each book provides material for about one term's work. **THE SKILLS OF FRIENDSHIP**, for example, is divided into thirteen chapters. Each chapter usually constitutes about one single-lesson period, and deals with one aspect of the skills of friendship.

The introductory section at the beginning of each book summarises the aims and contents of the strategies. This is followed by a 'Module Overview' which shows teachers, at a glance, the type of activity, what it aims to do, how long it should take, the size of the group, how many worksheets are available, whether additional materials are required and whether there are suggestions for developing or varying the strategy.

Within each chapter, 'Procedure' takes the teacher step-by-step through the exercise, and 'Notes' comment on the Procedure or highlight the purpose of the exercise.

# 10 HOW GOOD A FRIEND AM I?

**Aim:** To help students to a realistic perception of their friendship skills.

## Procedure:

- Form groups of 2–3.
- Give each student the worksheet **HOW GOOD A FRIEND AM I?**
- Read through the questionnaire and comment as necessary.
- Students are free to add questions of their own choice.
- Students complete their worksheets individually, asking help from the other group members if necessary.
- Students take it in turn to share the second part of the worksheet, i.e. I am a good friend because . . . and I could be a better friend by . . .

### Extension:
Give students several copies of **HOW GOOD A FRIEND AM I?** They are to ask a parent, teacher and friend to complete these about themselves. Then students compare their own perception of themselves with that of these chosen others.

**Group Size:** 2–3

**Time:** 20–30 minutes

**Materials:** Each student requires:
- worksheet **HOW GOOD A FRIEND AM I?**

## Notes:

In this strategy students assess themselves on the skills of friendship which have been identified and examined in this course. Some students may feel uncomfortable because of this and the teacher will need to be sensitive to students who may feel vulnerable. This exercise is to be seen in positive terms, a moment to give recognition to friendship skills as well as to draw attention to those skills requiring attention.

The questionnaire can be adapted by the teacher to cover other skill areas and is designed so that students can add questions of their own choice.

# HOW GOOD A FRIEND AM I?

Name _____  Date _____

**INVITE A FRIEND TO HELP YOU COMPLETE THIS QUESTIONNAIRE:**

| | ALWAYS | USUALLY | SOMETIMES | SELDOM | NEVER |
|---|---|---|---|---|---|
| Do I smile and make other people feel welcome? | | | | | |
| Do I get other people to talk about themselves and their interests? | | | | | |
| Do I listen really well? | | | | | |
| Do I make other people feel important? | | | | | |
| Do I say good things about others? | | | | | |
| Do I tease or belittle others? | | | | | |
| Do I argue a lot? | | | | | |
| Do I blame or talk about others behind their backs? | | | | | |
| Do I try and see life as other people see it? | | | | | |
| With someone I trust, do I share my personal thoughts and feelings? | | | | | |
| Do I ........................................... | | | | | |
| Do I ........................................... | | | | | |

I am a good friend because:

1 _____

2 _____

3 _____

I could be a better friend by:

1 _____

2 _____

3 _____

E.G. HOW WELL DO I LISTEN ....?

© Shay McConnon 1989

# 2 GROUP-BASED WORK

**YOUR CHOICE** emphasises experiential or participatory learning. This is a valuable way of learning about oneself and one's relationship with others. People can often learn more by doing than by watching or listening, and group-based work can lead to a deeper awareness and assessment of oneself and is a valuable way of experimenting with and practising new behaviours and skills.

The group can also be a stimulus for affective growth. This is particularly so when the group atmosphere is open, warm and friendly. When students feel personally valued by others, they tend to grow to value themselves and develop positive qualities. It is the teacher's task to create an atmosphere of trust and support, where students co-operate with and respect each other and where students are listened to and valued.

## Ground Rules

It can be useful in the early stages of a group's working life to invite the members to establish ground rules. This helps to ensure that students will be willing to listen to each other, and enables the teacher to share his or her concerns about group conduct. Students will probably commit themselves to their own rules more readily than to teacher-made rules.

The rules could be printed on a large sheet of paper and displayed in a prominent position in the room. They could also be reviewed from time to time. Sample rules:

— Only one person speaks at a time.
— Everyone listens to the speaker.
— No put-downs.
— Everyone is free to pass.

## Breaking into Groups

The strategies in **YOUR CHOICE** require students to work in groups of various sizes. Simply asking a large class to form working groups may cause problems, e.g. friendship patterns can dominate; people can be embarrassed and inhibited in making a decision on which group to join; and the 'orphaned' individuals whom nobody wants can find it a negative experience. Here are some ideas, therefore, for creating working groups of various sizes.

## Pairs

(a) This requires half as many pieces of string as there are students (the string should be the same colour and length). Hold the bundle of strings in your hand with the ends protruding on either side. Each student takes an end. Students are now 'strung together' in pairs.
(b) Make paired cards, e.g. Adam and Eve; Laurel and Hardy, etc. Shuffle the cards and give a card to each student, who has to find his or her partner. (Alternatively playing cards can be used as paired cards, e.g. the two red nines (hearts and diamonds).)

## Specific Number Groupings

(a) If you need a grouping of, for example, four groups of seven students, take four magazine pictures and cut each into seven pieces. Mix them together and give one piece to each student. Students group with those who have the other six pieces of the picture.
(b) Alternatively you could draw symbols on pieces of card — a different symbol for each group, with the number of cards with that symbol equalling the number of students required in that group. (Playing cards could be used instead.)

## Random Groupings

(a) Designate the four corners of the room to each of the four seasons. Students have to decide which is their favourite season and gather in that corner. The number of groups is determined by the number of choices given, e.g. two seasons instead of four will create two groups. Lots of variations are possible: birth signs, animals, food, music, colours, time of the day.
(b) Form groups of students who have the same colour eyes, hair, birth month, etc.

## To Mix Established Groupings

Ask students to form a line according to various criteria, e.g. a line from the shortest to the tallest, from the youngest to the oldest, using first names in alphabetical order, using birthdays from January to December, using house numbers. Break them into working groups once the line is formed, e.g. students could pair up with the person on their left. This enables the teacher to separate students who always work together.

# Types of Activities

Below is a list of the types of activities most frequently used in group work. Teachers will find that they can invent others, and the flexibility of the material will allow them to adapt the strategies as they wish.

## Brainstorming

This is an activity in which the teacher invites ideas, thoughts and beliefs on a specific topic without prior discussion. The rules are:

- Every idea offered is to be accepted.
- No criticism or evaluative comments are to be made.
- All contributions are to be written down quickly and briefly.
- The emphasis is on quantity not quality.

## Rank Ordering

In this activity students are invited to make a priority list of values, beliefs and opinions, etc. This can be an individual or a group task. The latter will require skills of negotiation and assertion. Rules might be:

- Listen to and understand the other person's viewpoint.
- Acknowledge the other person's viewpoint.
- Say where you stand.
- No sarcasm or put-downs.
- Be open to alternative ideas or solutions.
- To compromise is not to 'lose'.

## Role-Play

Role-play is an activity in which students are presented with a predetermined character and invited to 'become' that person in a given situation. Role-play will be helped by the following:

- Allow time for preparation.
- Get players to clarify and define their roles.
- Encourage the audience to be positive and supportive.
- Encourage a flexible approach and a sense of humour.
- Allow time to debrief.

## Rounds

This is an activity in which students form a circle facing each other and are given the opportunity to answer a question or complete a sentence. It is a good way to end a session. Rounds are helped by:

- Listening.
- Being honest.
- Being brief.
- The right to pass.

## Discussion

This activity provides students with the opportunity to express feelings and beliefs, to share others' perspectives and to clarify, modify and develop their own thinking. Discussion is helped by:

- Listening.
- A circle formation.
- Considering all contributions as worthwhile.
- The absence of put-downs.
- The involvement of the quieter members.
- The lack of dominating members.

## Scripted Fantasy

This is an invitation to explore experiences, feelings and beliefs through a guided, imaginary journey, experience or situation. Fantasy work is helped by:

- A clear, imaginative script, sensitively presented.
- A relaxed and secure environment.
- A receptive group.
- Avoidance of interruption or interpretation in the sharing process.

## Listening

Listening is an essential factor in good interpersonal communication. We often 'hear' but fail to 'listen'. It is a complex process demanding the awareness and practice of an amalgam of skills. Students need to acquire and practise these skills to ensure successful group work.

## Dos

- Look at the speaker.
- Adopt a relaxed and open body posture.
- Encourage the speaker to talk.
- Believe the speaker has something worthwhile to say.
- Smile and act in a friendly manner.
- Empathise.
- Reflect back what you have heard.

## Don'ts

- Interrupt.
- Blame/judge/advise.
- Fidget or look away.
- Dominate the conversation.
- Change the subject.

The teacher could make a poster showing the rules for brainstorming, rank ordering etc., then explain their importance to the students and display it for the duration of the course.

# Group Development

Students who have little experience of group work may need help to develop the interpersonal skills necessary for successful group work. This section contains a variety of standard activities, grouped under specific headings, which the teacher can use at any time to improve aspects of group functioning.

# Communication

These strategies offer awareness of and practice in simple communication procedures in both the sending and receiving of messages.

## Whispers

Group Size: 8–10

Time: 10 minutes

Materials: —

Procedure:
- Students form a circle.
- A sentence is whispered to one person who passes it around the circle until it gets back to the originator of the sentence.
- The original whisper is compared to the final whisper and distortions noted.
- Repeat this strategy and use it as an opportunity to practise listening and communicating accurately.

## Storytime

Group Size: 5–10

Time: 10 minutes

Materials: —

Procedure:
- Students form a circle and each is given a number.
- A volunteer makes up the first sentence of a story and calls out a number.
- The 'numbered' person paraphrases what has been said, adds another sentence, and calls out a third number.
- This continues until the story has a satisfactory ending.

## Follow Me

Group Size: Any number of pairs

Time: 10 minutes

Materials: Paper and pencils

Procedure:
- Students sit in chairs, back to back.
- A draws a picture and gives instructions to B who aims to draw the identical picture.
- After 2 minutes compare the results.
- Swap roles.

# Affirmation

These exercises are designed to help students feel good about themselves and good about the other members of the group.

## Pictures

Group Size: Any size then pairs

Time: 20 minutes

Materials: Large sheets of paper and markers

Procedure:
- Each student puts his name on the paper then draws an outline of himself (nothing artistic).
- Students then wander around the room writing positive comments within the outline about the person whose name is on the sheet.
- When this is done, students collect their sheets, read them quietly and circle the three most valued comments.
- Students form pairs to share and discuss the comments.

## You're OK Because . . .

Group Size: Pairs then groups of 4

Time        8 minutes

Materials:  —

Procedure:
- Form pairs.
- Each student has one minute to say as many positive things as possible as to why her partner is OK.
- Pairs join to form groups of 4 to discuss and share the experience.

## Circles

Group Size: 6–8

Time:       10 minutes

Materials:  —

Procedure:
- Each group forms a circle.
- One student volunteers to say something he likes about the person on his right.
- The student complimented now says something positive about the person on his right.
- This continues until everyone has had a say.
- This can be extended by students going round in the opposite direction.

# Co-operation

These exercises encourage co-operation and support among group members.

## Co-operative Musical Chairs

Group Size: Any size

Time:       Varies

Materials:  Chairs and music

Procedure:
- Set up as for the traditional musical chairs (two lines of chairs back-to-back).
- When the music stops it is the group's responsibility to see that no one is left standing — people can sit on each other's laps.
- Continue in the usual way, stopping music and removing chairs.
- Continue until it becomes unsafe to remove any more chairs.

## Help!

Group Size: Any size

Time:       Varies

Materials:  Small bean bags

Procedure:
- Each student wanders around the room balancing a bean bag on his or her head.
- The group can be asked to skip, hop, go backwards, sideways etc.
- If the bean bag falls off the student's head, he or she is frozen.
- This person is freed when another picks up the bean bag and replaces it on the frozen person's head.
- The group aims to keep all its members unfrozen.

## Alibis

Group Size: 6–8

Time:       20 minutes

Materials:  —

Procedure:
- A detective is chosen who makes up a crime and gives the group the details of where, when and how it was committed.
- The detective now stands in the middle of the group in order to cross-question the suspect. The group acts as that one suspect, remembering what each says and attempting to be consistent with answers.
- The detective turns to a student and begins the cross-examination. Then he quickly turns to another as if they were all the same person.
- The detective aims to catch out the suspect and break her alibi. When that happens because the reply is inconsistent, that person becomes the new detective and the game begins again.

# Trust

These activities can foster trust between group members. It is important that the atmosphere be as safe and as supportive as possible, and that these exercises be very carefully prepared and monitored.

## Blind Walk

Group Size: Pairs

Time:       Varies

Materials:  Blindfolds for half of the group

Procedure:
- Form pairs and decide who is to be blindfolded.
- The 'seeing' person leads her 'blind' partner through the room avoiding furniture, other people, etc.
- After a few minutes swap roles.

## Hop Aboard!

Group Size: 3

Time: 10–15 minutes

Materials: Blindfolds

Procedure:
- Two students form a seat with their hands and are blindfolded.
- The third person hops aboard and navigates the other two around, giving directions, avoiding other 'drivers', etc.
- Swap roles so each has the opportunity to become the 'driver'.

## Passing The Body

Group Size: 12+

Time: 10 minutes

Materials: —

Procedure:
- Form two lines of equal numbers with students facing each other about one metre apart.
- Each student crosses arms and holds hands with the person opposite. This forms a chain of hands along which a volunteer is passed from one end to the other with a rocking motion.
- Continue with other volunteers.

## Trust Circle

Group Size: 8–12

Time: 10 minutes

Materials: —

Procedure:
- Students form a tight circle facing inwards.
- A volunteer stands in the middle with eyes shut or blindfolded and falls towards the encircling members.
- The volunteer is supported and passed around the circle as gently and as smoothly as possible.

# Disclosure

These activities provide a structure for students to disclose ideas, feelings and experiences. No pressure should be put on students to share more than each feels comfortable about.

## Rounds

Group Size: 4–8

Time: 5–10 minutes

Materials: —

Procedure:
- The group forms a circle and each student takes it in turn to answer a question.
- Answers are to be brief and the other students are to listen without commenting.
- Everyone has the right to pass.
- Suggested questions:
  - What do you like about yourself?
  - What are you best at?
  - Why do people like you?
  - What have you learned today?

## Interviews

Group Size: Pairs then 8–12

Time: 10–15 minutes

Materials: —

Procedure:
- Students find a partner, preferably someone they don't know well.
- A interviews B and attempts to find out as much as possible in a minute.
- Reverse roles.
- In groups of 8–12, each student takes it in turn to introduce his partner, sharing the information acquired in the interview.

## Posters

Group Size: Any size

Time: 30 minutes

Materials: Poster-size paper, markers, blu-tack

Procedure:
- Each student is given a sheet of paper and writes her name on it.
- Students then use this paper to share with the group information about themselves, from hobbies to personality traits, to highly personal comments.
- Students can use words and/or drawings or be creative in some other way.
- Display the posters.

# Energisers

This section contains a number of activities that can be used to 'energise' and get a group working together. It is important to be selective in the use of energisers. They have a role to play in giving newly formed groups the experience of working together or when sessions go stale and need an injection of fun and energy.

## Mirror

Students form pairs facing each other. One takes the lead and the other performs a mirror image of the actions and facial expressions. After a few minutes they swap roles. This can be varied with a small group mirroring the actions of one person.

## Changes
A group of any size divides into two rows facing each other. Each carefully observes his partner. One row turns their backs, changes three things about their person (e.g. undoes a button) and then turns back. Each student has now to work out what three things his partner has changed.

## Killer
A group of 6 to 8 form a circle. By secret selection (drawing straws, cards, etc.) one member becomes the 'killer'. The 'killer' is to wink at her victims, making sure that the rest of the group do not see the wink. The victim is to die in a dramatic way. Anyone who thinks he knows the identity of the 'killer' is to make a challenge. If the challenge is wrong, that person drops out. If correct, the game ends and a new 'killer' is chosen. This can be varied by using other gestures besides winking as the 'killing' action.

## Ha Ha
A group of any size lies on the ground, side by side. The first person laughs 'ha' to the next person who says 'ha' and this is passed on down the line. Then the first person goes 'ha, ha' and so on down the line. Vary the pitch of the 'ha's'.

## Story
In a circle of 6 to 8, a volunteer begins a story with a single word. Each student takes it in turn to tell the story adding one word at a time. Keep this to a lively pace.

## Pyramid
Form groups of 4 to 8. Each group is to arrange itself so that there are only four feet on the ground. A time limit of 2 minutes can be set and the group must hold their position for 5 seconds. This can be varied with other challenges, e.g. two hands and two feet only on the ground.

## Dragon
In groups of 7, each member holds the waist of the person in front (with hands, not arms). The 'head' – the front person – tries to touch the 'tail' – the last person – while the 'body' tries to keep the 'tail' from being touched. At the end all the 'heads' of the various dragons chase and catch the 'tails' and the group ends up in a complete circle.

## Jungle Morning
Everyone stands, eyes closed, and pretends they are jungle animals. Dawn has arrived and the animals awaken. Softly at first, everyone makes the sound of their animal and gradually increases in volume. Animals can stretch as they wake up and when awake can walk round the 'jungle' greeting other animals.

## Blind Noises
In pairs, decide on a noise or sound by which each will recognise the other. Blindfolded, or with eyes closed, students move quietly about the room so that partners 'lose' each other. At a signal, each person makes the agreed noise and finds his partner.

## Human Pretzel
(For groups of 10+.) Two people leave the room. The others hold hands in a circle and then twist themselves over and under each other without letting go of hands. The two people outside the room come back in and 'untangle' the group.

## Farmyard
(For groups of 10+.) Each student is assigned an animal (there should be 2 or 3 of each animal). Pupils are to crawl around the room with eyes closed making the appropriate animal sounds and find the other animals of the same type.

## Human Noughts and Crosses
(For groups of 9+.) Arrange nine chairs as for noughts and crosses, i.e. three rows of three chairs spaced apart about three or four feet. One team is noughts and the other crosses. Call out noughts and the first nought runs to a chair of her choice and sits with arms circled above her head. Call out crosses and the first cross runs and sits in a chair of his choice with arms crossed on the chest. Alternate teams are called until one team wins. The rules are the same as for paper noughts and crosses.

# Difficulties

Successful group work is not always easy to achieve. It takes great skill on the part of the teacher, as well as tact, humour and patience, and it depends on the willingness of the group members to participate and co-operate. This is not always the case. The solution lies in the teacher's ability to cope creatively with each situation. Teachers must use their own resourcefulness and a personal repertoire of techniques and skills. Success requires that they have such a repertoire, and the skill and stamina to cope with problems as they arise. This section looks at some difficulties that may arise and offers hints on how to cope with them.

# Students Who Dominate

Group work is often hampered by students who dominate, interrupt or fail to listen. Here are some activities that can regulate contributions from group members.

## The Conch

Materials: Anything that can be easily passed round a group, e.g. bean bag, ruler, ball etc.

Procedure:
- Only when holding the conch is one allowed to speak.
- To obtain the conch, students must raise their hands and wait for it to be passed to them.
- Conditions may be imposed, e.g. no one may hold the conch a second time until all the other members of the group have contributed should they wish to do so.

## P.A.Y.S. (Pay As You Speak)

Materials: Tokens

Procedure:
- Each group member is given a number of tokens.
- Every time a person speaks it costs one token which is collected by a 'banker'.
- Students are not allowed to contribute once their tokens have been spent.

## Observation

Materials: Checklist and marker

Procedure:
- An observer is appointed who makes out a simple chart with a list of the group members' names.
- Whenever someone contributes to the discussion, the observer ticks that name.
- Making students aware of how they can dominate a group in this objective way, can sometimes bring its own controls.
- The results of the observation can be brought to the group's attention and the problem actively resolved by the group.

# Students Who Disrupt

Students who behave in disruptive ways usually do so for a specific reason; there is usually some 'pay-off' for them. It will help to analyse what this might be. Practically the situation can be helped by:
- Talking to the student out of class to try to understand his or her behaviour and feelings and discover a more acceptable way of achieving this 'pay-off'.
- Focusing the group's attention on to the disruptive behaviour and inviting the group to resolve the problem.
- Involving the disruptive person with a specific task, e.g. an observation role.

# Students in Conflict

When the discussion gets polarised, invite the students involved to sit facing each other in the middle of the group. The students continue their argument but, before each can reply to the other, each has to paraphrase what the other student has just said — to that other student's satisfaction. This activity encourages students to listen to and focus on each other's points of view.

# 3 THE ROLE OF THE TEACHER

The teacher is central to the success of this programme. Her role is diverse – structuring the learning experiences, facilitating groups and modelling personal skills and qualities.

## The Teacher as Model

In so far as it is possible, create a relaxed working atmosphere where students will be free to be open, honest and supportive of each other. Be prepared to participate and join in the various activities e.g. fill in worksheets and questionnaires and share these with the class.

Students will see the teacher as a model for behaviours, attitudes and values. Teachers who display positive attitudes and sensitivity can engender similar behaviours within the group.

## The Central Belief

Central to the success of this programme is the belief that each person is important, of value and to be listened to. A vital role of the teacher is to help students to this belief of themselves and of each other.

## The Right to Pass

Students should feel free to opt out of those activities where they feel vulnerable or at risk. Generally they will want to take part in groups where students are positive and supportive in their relationships with each other.

## Listening

Listening is a fundamental interpersonal skill and young people are not always aware of its importance. It is very important to successful group work. Ensure that students have equal time to talk and, if necessary, use some of the techniques for regulating contributions in discussion (see p. 9).

## Observation

The teacher should try to be aware of what is going on in the different groups and when necessary give his attention to individuals or to one of the working groups. This may be to clarify procedure, to keep a group on task, to encourage shy people to participate or to deal with disruptive or noisy students.

## Closing A Session

Allow time at the end of a session for students to reflect and share what has been learnt. This can be a moment to reinforce specific teaching points and resolve any difficulties that may exist. Closing a session like this can settle a class before students move to another teacher.

## Time

The time given for each strategy is to be considered approximate and the teacher should monitor the groups' working pace to decide how long any one activity should last.

## Display

The teacher might like to encourage students to make use of wall space for posters, worksheets etc. Invite a group to take responsibility for displaying work connected with the programme.

## Video Camera

There are many moments when the use of a video camera would be useful. To record and play back students' behaviours can be an important learning moment for the students.

## Facilitating Groups

This course involves dividing a class of 30+ pupils into smaller working groups. The teacher could introduce some of the students to simple group-work techniques. They can then act as 'leaders' within the groups, encouraging participation, listening, constructive criticism and positive feedback.

## Recording

Recording is an important element in the course and most strategies have accompanying worksheets which require completion by the students. It is recommended that these be kept in individual files.

# Questions and Answers

## 'I have no experience in active learning methods and I lack confidence.'

Begin slowly. Try a safe activity with a class with whom you have a good working relationship, e.g. Situations (**THE SKILLS OF FRIENDSHIP** p. 7). Or try one of the group development activities listed in this guide as part of a more traditional lesson. You may be surprised to find that your students enjoy active learning.

Alternatively, attend courses on experiential learning. In this way the teacher can experience these methods at first hand and become familiar and confident with this approach.

## 'How do I cope with a noisy group?'

The methods used in this course do involve student interaction and hence noise! If the noise level is of concern to you, draw the students' attention to this and seek their help in resolving the problem. You may find it useful to use some of the techniques for regulating contributions in discussion (see p. 9).

## 'I don't want my students arriving at another class excited and noisy.'

Students who have shown a lot of energy and interacted in a lively way, may need to quieten down before changing classes, so most strategies conclude with a reflective moment. This is usually in the form of a discussion and, where appropriate, there are suggestions for discussion topics in each strategy. Rounds (p. 4) will also be a helpful way to close a session.

## 'How do I cope with colleagues who are critical of this approach?'

Teachers who are critical might be feeling threatened by new ideas and teaching methods. Those teachers who suffer criticism can feel isolated and begin to doubt themselves. There is no easy answer to this. Here are a few ideas, however, that might help.

Talk to colleagues and try to create pockets of support and/or acceptance for what you are doing. Seek recognition from senior staff. Show how active learning methods benefit other subject areas. Invite colleagues to sit in and observe or take part in a session.

## 'I'm afraid my pupils might not see this as "real work".'

Comments like, 'We only play games and don't learn much' can give the wrong impression of participatory learning. Be clear yourself about your objectives, and let the students know what these are and maybe invite them to assess whether or not these have been achieved. The learning dimension to the course can be emphasised by concluding sessions with Rounds (see p. 4), e.g. 'Today I learnt that . . .'.

In this course there are opportunities for work of a 'traditional' nature and the teacher may wish to extend the use of written and homework assignments to overcome a concern that students may see this as a time when they just 'play games'.

## 'How can I explain to my pupils what this programme is about?'

The following analogy might help. 'Life is like a game of football or netball. You can't play well until you know how to control, pass and shoot the ball. In life we can't play well (be a success) unless we know how to speak, listen, feel good about ourselves and others and get along with people. We are not born with these skills. Successful people have made themselves successful. This course provides an opportunity to learn about these skills, to practise them and to check out with others how successful we are in using these skills.'

# BOOKLIST

This list of books is in two parts. The first list contains books that mainly cover the background and theory of personal growth and effectiveness. The second list contains activities that can be used in the classroom. Obviously there is an overlap as some of the titles provide both theory and practical exercises.

## Theoretical

**Becoming A Person** by C. Rogers, Constable, 1967.
**A Guide to Student-Centred Learning** by D. Brandes and P. Ginnis, Basil Blackwell, 1986.
**I'm OK, You're OK** by T. Harris, Pan, 1973.
**Lifeskills Teaching** by B. Hopson and M. Scally, McGraw-Hill, 1981.
**New Teaching Skills** by N. Collins, Oxford University Press, 1986.
**People Making** by V. Satir, Condor (London), 1978.
**Personal, Social and Moral Education** by B. Wakeman, Lion, 1984.
**Social Skills and Personal Problem Solving** by P. Priestly, J. McGuire and D. Flegg, Tavistock, 1978.
**The Teacher and Pastoral Care** by D. H. Hamblin, Basil Blackwell, 1978.
**Why Am I Afraid to Love?** by J. Powell, Argus Communications (Illinois), 1967.
**Why Am I Afraid to Tell You Who I Am?** by J. Powell, Argus Communications (Illinois), 1969.
**Working with Groups** by A. Satow and M. Evans, Tacade (Manchester), 1983.
**You and Me** by G. Egan, Brooks/Cole (Monterey, California), 1977.

## Practical

**100 Ways to Enhance Self-Concept in the Classroom** by J. Canfield and H. Wells, Prentice-Hall, 1976.
**Active Tutorial Work** by J. Baldwin and H. Wells, Basil Blackwell, 1979.
**Choices** by D. Settle and C. Wise, Basil Blackwell, 1986.
**Creative Communication and Community Building** by W. Rice, J. Roberto and M. Yaconelli, St Mary's Press (Minnesota), 1981.
**Gamesters' Handbook** by D. Brandes and H. Phillips, Hutchinson Education, 1979.
**Gamesters Two** by D. Brandes, Hutchinson Education, 1982.
**Group Tutoring for the Form Teacher** by L. Button, Hodder & Stoughton, 1982.
**Learning from Experience** by C. Barnett, R. Chambers and K. Longman, Macmillan, 1985.
**Lifeskills Teaching Programmes 1, 2, 3 and 4** by B. Hopson and M. Scally, Lifeskills Associates (Leeds), 1979, 1982, 1986, 1988.
**Self-Esteem: A Classroom Affair** by M. and C. Borba, Winston Press (Minneapolis), 1978.
**Simulations** by C. Barnett, R. Chambers and K. Longman, Macmillan, 1986.
**Windows to Our Children** by V. Oaklander, Real People Press (Utah), 1978.